Zombies at the Door

Planning for the Inevitable

Charles M. Pulsipher

Zombies at the Door
Planning for the Inevitable

Copyright © 2011 Charles M. Pulsipher
Cover design by Charles M. Pulsipher
Artwork by Charles M. Pulsipher
First Publication: September 1st 2011

Published by: Singular Books

This is a work of fiction. Names, characters, places, zombies, and incidents are products of the author's imagination and are used fictitiously.

No part of this book may be used, reproduced, or transmitted in any manner without written permission, except in the case of brief quotations for critical articles and reviews. All rights reserved.

Printed in the United States of America.

To my friend, Adam.

When I think of zombies, I think of you.

Introduction

(skip this if it's an actual emergency)

I wrote this originally as a gag Christmas gift for my friends and family. I wanted it to be funny, but still supply people with valuable life-saving information that could be applied to any disaster scenario.

Zombies, earthquakes, floods, fires, solar storms, alien invasion, electromagnetic pulses that knock out power, and pandemics…yeah, this thing is made to help and entertain you in the process.

I printed over a dozen copies and gave away around ten. The others disappeared within two months as people begged for copies. I decided I needed to give this gag gift to the world.

You're welcome.

Note: This is not meant to replace any actual plans you may have for emergencies or any directions you receive from the government, military, and law enforcement. If it saves your life, then it has done so to the surprise of the writer and everyone else.

The writer in no way condones theft, looting, vandalism, zombie tagging, raising of ruckuses, stealing, rioting, robbery, misappropriation of food, goods, or merchandise, seizing of tanks, bazookas, and grenades, or the murdering of innocent people who just have a regular disease and not the incurable zombiepox.

In a Zombie Emergency Read This First

Okay, it happened. I knew it would. We knew it would. No surprise really. That's why you have this guide, you saw what was coming. You're smart...ish.

You were brushing your teeth this morning, picking at that annoying ingrown hair while the television ran in the background, just like every other day. But, today you heard the word "zombie" drift in from the other room, clear as day.

"Shzomby?" you repeated back to yourself in the mirror, toothbrush dangling from the corner of your mouth. It fell to the sink and you ran out to turn up the volume on your beautiful flat screen (that has now become as useless as your underwear).

Videos of fire, destruction, and shuffling masses appeared on the screen. You squealed like a three year old girl at a princess party just for her. When you calmed down, you scrambled over to the bookshelf or your ereader and pulled this down.

Good for you! Seriously! That was some level headed thinking in this time of panic and distress. I mean, there are plenty of good books there, but that sparkly vampire or that wizard with glasses isn't going to be much help today, now is he?

What To Do

Take a moment to collect yourself. Breathe deeply, hold, release. Count to five, not ten. You don't have time for ten! What are you even thinking *ten* for?!! Stop that. Ten doesn't exist…five and five only. You have a lot of work to do, so focus already. Reached five yet? Good, let's get to it.

<u>Important</u>: DO NOT PANIC and DON'T YOU DARE SCREAM! We will forgive the initial squeal. That was understandable, but no more. Screaming is the equivalent of wafting the scent of freshly cooked bacon over a sleeping fat man to a zombie. Got it? Screaming = Zombie Bacon.

I like mine crispy!

Bacon sounds good now. I wish I had some. Dang you for bringing it up! Stupid bacon. Anyway…scream and they'll come running, stumbling, and slobbering for your sweet breads in a heartbeat. Don't scream!

Mmmm…bacon. Sounds really good now, doesn't it? I blame you. Crisp and salty on eggs over toast. Wait. Am I drooling a little?

Drooling?! That reminds me. Wipe your mouth! That toothpaste dribbling down your chin is going to get you shot if you aren't careful. Clean now? Good. That was a close one.

Go and slowly, quietly close your blinds and bolt your doors. Zombies are like little children. If they don't see you or hear you, you don't exist.

Oh, and find yourself a weapon: gun, axe, shovel, hatchet, baseball bat, stick with nail, table leg, etc. You don't want to be relying on your two fists right now. Zombies bite fists, and fingers, and arms, and…well you get the idea.

Not for a quick bath.

Next, fill up all your tubs with water. This is critical. If you have to shelter in place for a while, you'll need it. Water is one of the big advantages you will have over your zombie food neighbors if you're smart and listen to me.

If you've managed to accomplish all this without getting your brains eaten, then you're probably better off than most of the population. Nice job. I'm glad too. It really would've been difficult for you to keep reading if you were a zombie.

Get Help

Time to call your friends. Be aware that some of them may be zombies by now. This doesn't mean you hang up if they answer "grrrr, arrrgh, yarhhg, or eeerrr!" Give them a moment to wake up, just in case they're still somewhat comatose from a long night of whatever your friends do and not a zombie. Or they could still be in shock that this happened, even though any friend of yours should have seen it coming.

If the grunting and moaning continues for several minutes, hang up. Let them go, they're not going to be helpful any longer. If you enjoy the company of the biting, drooling, and brain eating undead, go ahead and keep them on the phone for a while, but I in no way endorse this kind of fraternization with zombies.

Phone Numbers

You should have a list of much needed phone numbers and addresses written in this book. If this is an ereader, I hope you jotted them down somewhere. These will be a lifeline in this troubled time. Please remember that telephone lines may be flooded.

Everyone will be trying to call their personal lifelines, mothers, and psychic friends right now. You can often get a text message through when cell phone lines are busy. You can also use a pay phone when nothing else seems to work.

Know where payphones are! They are usually in high traffic areas that you will want to avoid, so know where the offbeat ones are. 911 will be useless, inundated with calls from zombie victims who think that the police will actually be able to help. Like they train the local PD for a zombie infestation. For some unknown reason this important scenario has not been added to their training dockets.

Also, make sure you write down those names, phone numbers, and addresses <u>before</u> the zombie plan is necessary! There's space at the back of this thing. And, keep it up to date. Seriously, you can be a little lazy sometimes. And, write down land lines if they've got them!

Meet and Greet

Once you've contacted all your non-zombie friends and relatives, it's time to form a convoy and group up. Some zombie plans will tell you to go it alone. That's a bad idea.

The more people you have around you, the higher probability that the zombies will get them instead of you…um…I would tell them something else though. Strength in numbers! We have to stick together to make it through this! We'll watch each other's backs! Something like that will motivate them. Don't refer to them as targets or distractions.

Throw your 72 hour kit in your car, add nonperishable food from your pantry, and as much water as you can, along with a few choice weapons. Have bottles of soda or juice? Empty them and fill them with water. You'll thank me later. Now let's meet up with all the spare targets (friends) you can find.

If you don't have a 72 hour kit, you'd better hope someone has a 144 hour kit. Once again, don't be so lazy and get a 72 hour kit together <u>beforehand!</u> Oh, a First Aid Kit might be a good idea too. You should have one in your 72 Hour Kit, but, obviously, you're lazy, so it's a bit of a crap shoot, isn't it? (See Appendix 1-A for an example 72 Hour Kit and Appendix 1-B for an example First Aid Kit)

What are you still doing reading this? It's time to go. Your friends are waiting. Go, Go, Go!

Meeting Places

So you've talked to your friends and family members who haven't upgraded their vocabulary with "Yarrrghh." Your car is packed, but where are you going? Hopefully that was part of your conversation with your friends. If not, well you have some redialing to do there, genius! Meeting somewhere safe will allow you to group for strength in numbers (wink, wink), allowing the zombies to pick you off one by one. Here is a list of possible meeting places:

The Old Abandoned Whatever Building

Every town has them. The old grocery store or mill or insane asylum or creepy hospital up on the hill. Despite the creepy vibe of old abandoned buildings, this is always a good spot to meet and decide what to do next or where to go. That building most likely isn't being used (hence being called abandoned) and all your friends know where it is from your obsessive driving past it and pointing out the creepiness. I don't recommend the asylum though, but that might just be the video games I've played talking.

Truck Rentals

Truck rentals are a great place during a zombie attack. A rental truck is designed to be driven by any moron with a driver's license (like you). They're well built and can take a little wear and tear. The trucks come in a multitude of sizes.

I recommend the middle size truck, with better gas mileage than the bigger ones, but enough room for quite a few people and supplies. Each truck is also sitting on the lot gassed up and ready to go. The keys are either inside a flimsy drop box on the side of the building or inside the flimsy building itself (often a trailer). I don't recommend stealing, but the undead are walking the streets. Leave an I Owe You or a credit card.

Friend's Cabin or Property Out of Town

Now you're thinking! A great place if everyone knows how to get there. You just have to be careful on the approach. If your friend's family beat you there, you may get shot for trespassing. Prod your friend out in front with a stick and make him/her explain to his/her hillbilly cousins that they need you and your group of friends. Point out the rental truck full of goodies, but imply that your keen mind, thanks in no small part to my guide, may save them all.

Ranch, Dead, or Unfinished Exits

Many parts of the country have freeway exits that aren't in use. These are usually far from a central location, but they make up for this flaw with several great features. They're close to the freeway with easy access for you, your friends, and the big truck you...borrowed. They're fairly deserted most days, so less zombies to get in the way of your planning. They're not someplace many others will think of...unless I sell a lot of these. Don't worry about that. I'm sure that won't happen.

Ranch exits often lead to miles of back country and dirt roads. Dead exits are a great place to do some quick meeting and planning before you take off for someplace better. Unfinished exits often lead to half finished roads that may take you somewhere safe...ish like new and empty complexes under construction.

Individual Homes

If you're unable to contact someone by phone, you may be tempted to swing by their home to check on them. This is courageous and heartwarming, especially if I'm one of the ones you were unable to contact. But, this is also extremely dangerous and a little stupid, unless you're getting me. Then it is only brave. I mean, I wrote this thing, you owe me, right?

Keep in mind, you're entering the heart of the population and getting further and further away from the main roads leading out of town as you head to someone's house. It's risky. I'm not suggesting you abandon someone (like me), but get in and get out as fast as possible. Don't linger too long and don't designate a home as a meeting place.

Homes aren't really designed to withstand zombies. They were built to withstand some light rain, maybe a little wind, some kid throwing a very small stick, but not zombies. I don't know why architects don't take this kind of thing into account, but few ever do. Sad really.

Is a zombie day like a snow day?

A School

This is only a good option if it's not a school day. You don't want to stumble into a bunch of angst-ridden, teenage zombies. Not only will they want to bite you and eat your brains, but they'll be whiny and bratty while doing so.

Once again, if you have to swing by to get a loved one, be quick and don't stick around. If it's a weekend, the summer, or a holiday, this may be a good choice for a quick meeting zone. A zombie will instinctively steer away from schools on a day off.

Trust me, it's science. Deep down they won't want to go near a school during the summer, Christmas, Thanksgiving, etc. Just be aware, if it's a weekend, you may have a few extra-curricular zombies show up and then the others will arrive in droves on Monday. On the flip side, bars and clubs are a bad place to be on the weekends and St. Patrick's Day.

Grocery Stores or Big Box Stores

Seems like a good idea, doesn't it? You're dead wrong. Bad idea. Everyone else will do the same, running to buy milk and bread like that'll stave off zombies. Dumb people. They're walking into a trap.

Half the people that work in these stores are half zombie on a good day. Just hearing that the zombie infestation has begun will send them over the edge into full zombitude (it's a word, I swear). You'd be walking into a nightmare, clutching your bread and milk, fighting with other customers who can't drive their carts.

When you make your way to the front at least you'll get to know that the zombie who'll be eating you today is "Susan" and she has "3 Years of Service" before she knocks that precious bread and milk from your hands and bites into your brain.

The Mall

No, No, No! BAD IDEA. Did movies teach you nothing? Does the mall ever help anyone survive?

If you're still debating this, here are the reasons why not: too many people, not much food, lots of dead ends, the building as a whole is not designed to keep people or zombies out, and instinct will drive zombies here in mass.

A zombie's brain doesn't work right. They know they need something, but can't remember what that thing is until they have a human in front of them. Then the light bulb comes on. "Oh yeah…brains…mmmm….brains."

Where do people go when they need something, but can't remember what? The mall! I don't even want to think what would happen if Zombie Day and Black Friday ever aligned. Can you imagine it? Gives me chills.

The Roof of Such and Such Building

This is clever. I'm surprised you thought of it. Oh yeah, you didn't. I just gave it to you. You're welcome again.

Flat roofs are a good place to meet. You can see everyone heading your way. You can pick off the occasional zombie as it chases one of your friends. Zombies are also notoriously bad climbers. It doesn't matter if they were gymnasts, rock climbers, or parkour champions, once zombified they cannot climb. Pull your rental truck right up to the ladder and you also have a quick get-away.

Destinations

Get Out

This is no particular destination at all, just a mad dash out of town and as far away as possible. This is the only destination you should have in mind if the zombie infestation is localized to your town and not national or global.

You don't want to be there if that's the case. Forget the mall, forget the rental truck, get in your car and go. A fire bomb or nuke could already be on its way. Go, go, go!

Shelter in Place

This isn't really the best option, but you may end up stuck with it if you're unlucky or you don't move fast enough. As I mentioned earlier homes, apartments, and condos are just not designed to keep out zombies. It comes in handy for other problems though, say a nice normal pandemic.

But, if you're surrounded and there's no way out without having to blunder through thousands of the drooling undead, then…well…this is the only instance you should stay put during a zombie infestation. Stay quiet. Keep the blinds down and closed. Barricade the doors and windows. Keep lights to a minimum, not the best time for a rave party or to be testing out that new surround sound system.

Use the food in your fridge first. You do not know how long the electricity will last, if it's still working at all (Do not use food that has already gone bad from your neglect of leftovers. Now is not the time to get sick).

If the electricity is out, use the perishable food within the first day. That doesn't mean start shoveling cheese, milk, and ice cream down your throat. Take it easy. Eat what you can. Move frozen food to a cooler along with vegetables and meats from your fridge. There is one sure fire way to keep your food from spoiling and it's what the professionals use, heat.

Hopefully you have a little gas stove in your 72 hour kit. Fill a pan with your frozen and fresh veggies, meats, tomato sauces, etc. Add some water and bring it to a simmer. That's it. If you keep food at a simmer it will not grow bacteria and you will not die eating it. I can't guarantee it will taste amazing. Use those herbs and spices you usually ignore in that rack next to the stove.

Your gas will run out. If you have a fireplace, then you're better off than me. Break down your furniture and keep that soup hot. Then move on to your cupboards and pantries. Anything veggie or meat related that you cannot finish in one meal goes into the soup. Finally you'll turn to your 72 hour kits or food storage. Most homes have several weeks' worth of food floating around if you're not being too picky. Believe me, now is not the time to be picky.

Water will be a problem. You don't know how long that will last or if it's been contaminated with zombie cooties. You **DO NOT** want zombie cooties. That's why I had you fill up the bath tub.

As long as you have electricity, use any liquids in your fridge first (see note above). Then move on to your bathtub water. I recommend boiling it. It won't have much in the way of bacteria, but it will pick up some from your funky tub, more if you are as lazy as the patterns seem to say.

Toilet water next, the water in the tank, not the bowl (Note: do not drink this if you used some sort of cleaning tablet. Otherwise, lap it up). Then your water heater. Turn it off first if you still have electricity. I recommend boiling these too, just in case the zombie plague reached the water supply. Last, your 72 hour kit or food storage water. This should keep you well hydrated for a while. Hopefully you won't run out, someone comes for you soon, or the zombies disperse enough for you to escape.

Distribution Center

This isn't available in all locations, but many towns have a big box distribution center. This is the ultimate supply depot. They have everything you could dream of needing during a zombie infestation. Food, water, camping gear, and more.

Once again, I don't condone stealing, but zombies are trying to eat you and your friends. Leave another I Owe You or credit card.

This could get tricky. These places have many workers and drivers heading in and out all day. Hope the news has made them all panic and abandon their posts well before you get there. And pray none of them are zombies, waiting inside.

You have a couple options once there. The roof of the distribution center may be a good place to set up camp in a pinch. I would recommend going somewhere far away from zombies (and their food, people) that can be fortified for defense, but if travel becomes difficult, the roof is a good option.

You can easily haul whatever you need up there. These buildings are huge, massive, and also big. You can see them from space (almost). I may exaggerate a little, but they're definitely big enough that you won't be visible from the ground. Remember, you don't exist if zombies can't see you.

Dozens of people could live on the roof in makeshift homes and tents. Food, water, and supplies would be within a quick scavenger hunt at any time as you wait out the zombies (Note: scavenger hunts are more fun without the zombies).

The other option is to load up all you can carry and head somewhere else. If you met up at truck rental building first, then you have a medium sized truck ready to fill up with all the gear and supplies you need. If not, you should at least have several cars. Just avoid the zombies hiding in the massive warehouse.

Once loaded, there are plenty of out of the way places you can end up with your cargo (aka booty) that will be suitable for survival. Just please don't take it to the mall!

Lakes and Reservoirs

Anywhere you end up, you need water. Always remember that, especially if you live in a desert, not to be confused with dessert, which can be nice.

Lakes and reservoirs have a large supply of water. You want the ones that are hard to get to and well away from population centers, not the water park in the middle of town or the splash pad down the street.

You may have issues with the locals who try to shoot anything zombie-ish (also a word). Try not to be zombie-ish. You should always boil water that may have had zombies or anything else not so pleasant in it. Zombies do enjoy a nice wade every now and again. Not big swimmers though.

Remote Valleys or Canyons

These are great if they're not well known. If they're tourist traps, you'll be fighting plenty of other people for the best places to hide and hole up.

This is always a pity that you have to fight other normal humans when there are plenty of zombies that require your attention. Why can't we all just get along?

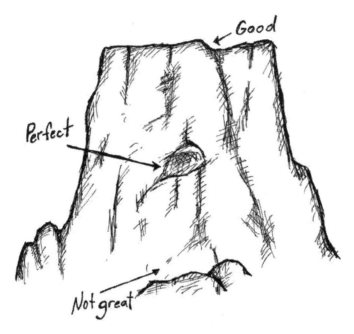

Canyon floors are not always the best place to be. Think higher, harder to climb to. A large ledge or cave halfway up a cliff could make a nice new home. Make a rope ladder to get friends up and down and a slanted roof so any zombie falling from above will slide off. Zombies don't sound like raindrops when they fall. Expect some loud, thumping nights.

Make sure you have access to water. Springs, streams, rivers, snowmelt, something. Remote cabins can be fortified with your gear from the distribution center. Make sure you bring plenty of weapons and food.

Forests

These are usually fairly remote which is great. Find water and build some good tree houses. You'll be fine. Just don't get lost. Moss grows on the North side of trees. That doesn't help if you don't know which direction your tree fort is though, so just don't get lost in the first place. That makes everything easier. Getting lost in a dark forest with zombies is not my idea of a good time.

Forests are also home to a lot of edibles. Look for game trails and tie nooses along them. Don't be afraid to eat something that you normally wouldn't. There might be an occasional feral pig out there, but there's not much bacon in the forest.

Worms and grasshoppers aren't too bad when you're starving. Just make sure you cook them well. Tape worms are not your friends even when you aren't running from the undead. Many plants are poisonous. Only use plants you can identify as safe and edible. When in doubt, don't risk it.

Mountain Property

These can be extremely remote and not well known. Don't go to the resort where everyone has a time share. That's not the mountain property I'm talking about.

The good ones often have plenty of snowmelt, springs, ponds, and streams. But, they may have no buildings or sometimes just a broken down trailer for protection. You can use your truck as a base camp until you can build more permanent living situations.

Try not to get shot by locals or people who beat you there first. It can be near impossible to get to these places in a rental truck if it's raining or snowing. Wolves and other predators may keep zombies from getting too close. This is a fairly good option if you can get the truckload of supplies up there and, if you manage to swing by a home improvement store beforehand, even better.

Prison

This is a last ditch option if you're unable to get out of town. Hopefully, most of the inmates are dumb enough to escape and scatter in the chaos of brain biting zombiness, leaving the place practically empty.

Empty is good. Full of inmates is bad. Full of criminal zombies with a history of violence before they decided that your head meat tasted good, even worse. Yet, a prison is a very easy place to defend with all that razor wire, fences, and bars. It should have a nice stockpile of food and water too. I'd start a garden in one of the exercise fields. It would be very quaint and domestic.

Military Depot

This sounds like a good place to set up camp. It very well might be. Just know that some jumpy new recruit with his nervous about zombies trigger finger is waiting just on the other side of that fence. He could just pop anything that moves.

Approach slowly with a white flag in the middle of the day while blasting some soothing music on your boom box. That may help.

Yes, tanks, bazookas, and grenades sound good right about now. I don't blame you for wanting big tough people with guns between you and the zombie horde. Just be careful. Big tough people with guns make for the worst zombies.

Reinforced Windowless Buildings

Concrete and steel, few to no windows, generators, solar panels, bathrooms, and more. These buildings are hard to come by, but they're out there. Keep an eye out and make mental notes of where you see them. These are great places to bunker down. They are often for large scale computing or manufacturing. Just know that some are near impossible to get into in the first place.

Avoid

Super Markets/Grocery Stores/Big Box Stores

These will be a looting, frantic mess. They'll also be a breeding ground for zombies. You may be tempted to go looking for supplies, but there are better places, like the distribution centers and warehouses.

Normal people are driven to snap at others while navigating the aisles with their carts and screaming spawn under the best conditions. What do you expect from zombies?

Also, I have my suspicions that these stores may be the source of the zombie strain. Next time you're in one, just look at the employees (sorry anyone I may know who works or has worked at such a store). They're practically zombies already.

Schools/Hospitals/Universities

Any place with a high population is not where you want to be right now (sorry anyone who works in a school, hospital, or university). Get out and stay out.

Remote is good. People close enough to bite you is not ideal. Once again, schools would be okay on a holiday, but universities don't always follow this rule. Hospitals are bad because zombies will instinctively be drawn to them. They aren't well and part of them knows that. Unless they are like me and then they'll be drawn toward the quackery they sell in herb and vitamin shops. Just another reason to avoid the mall.

Malls

Malls never will be a good place to avoid zombies. I feel I can't cover this enough. Too many people, too much glass, not really much food or water. Zombies enjoy malls, amusement parks, movie theaters, and anyplace that their subconscious associates with fun, pleasure, and fondness.

The problem is zombies bite when they feel pleasure, fun, or fondness. Not to mention Hollywood has taught us that you'll eventually run out of supplies, turn on each other, be overrun, and die horribly. So avoid the mall if at all possible.

Zombies

Yeah…this is obvious. Zombies want to eat you. Avoid being eaten. Use those shovels, axes, guns, fire, flares, petroleum jelly, ammonia, paper bags, and whatever else works.

Run, hide, jump, climb, drive, walk briskly, but do not skip. Zombies are drawn to skipping…or was that flying monkeys? Climbing is always a good option. Zombies lack the dexterity to climb or play video games well. Doesn't stop them from trying, but don't worry, they'll fail at both.

Stairs slow them down, but really are not much of a problem for them, but trees, poles, buildings, rocks, and other climbable objects are a great way to get away. Get on a roof and take out a section of the stairs and you can wait comfortably without fear. Just remember, zombies can wait a long time for you to come back down. Try to find someplace where you are not visible and they'll forget you were ever there.

Dentist Offices

Chewing on people does a number to your teeth. Zombies will file into dentist offices in mass. When they find no one to help their rotten, chipped, and broken teeth, they'll want to chew on more people. Ironic, I know, but zombies don't really understand irony or care that you find it funny as they sink down to their gums in your forearm.

Killing Friends

I don't know about you, but I try not to kill my friends. This is a pretty good idea if you want to have friends in the first place. Zombie infestation makes this more difficult, but not impossible.

If your friend gets bitten, don't immediately lunge at them with your makeshift machete. The transformation isn't instantaneous, despite what some movies would have you believe. You don't really know how it works either. Your friend could be immune and then there goes the miracle cure for us all in an impulsive hatchety mess.

Does it matter that no one's been immune yet? Nope, it only takes one.

If they do turn, let them go to wander around as long as you can safely release them to frolic with their fellow zombies. If not, lock them up somewhere. What if we do find a cure? I'm fairly sure it won't work on dismembered zombies. Even if it did, who wants that?

Oh, and if you get bitten, repeat "friends are friends, not food" over and over again. Maybe you can be the first zombie to not attack your friends, or better yet, attack other zombies. That would be nice of you.

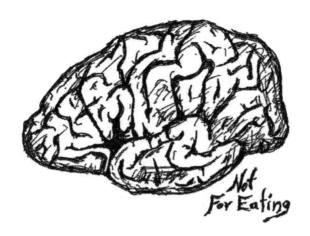

Brains are pretty!
No wonder zombies like them.

Other Places of Interest

Pawn Shops

These are a great place to pick up a few weapons. You can find guns, power tools, chainsaws, and any number of useful items, even swords. I so want a sword. You should too. Pawn shop owners won't take too kindly to looters, so I'd bring some cash or some food to barter with.

Abandoned Buildings/Warehouses

Great place to hide if forced into a corner and unable to get out. Warehouses can be full of food, water, supplies, camping gear, or worthless junk. You have to go in and find out. Though they can be a little frightening and have lead to disaster in many a video game and super creepy movie. You better have a good flashlight and try not to think about that movie with zombie vampires.

Baseball Diamonds

Everyone knows zombies love baseball. Start a game and they will shuffle to the stands and watch enthralled. This will give you priceless minutes to escape.

Sorry anyone who loves baseball, but it's just so boring. It's almost too boring to use this plan, but to save myself from zombies I'll use even this. It is also very difficult to accomplish without a ball and bat.

Yawn!

DMV

Zombies will instinctively line up here, waiting for their number to be called. They will mill around moaning impatiently. Skip the line, jump the counter, and escape out the back. Just avoid any zombies working behind the counter. They may not be happy about the crowds you just brought in with you.

So Angry...

Airport

I don't know how to pilot anything not associated with a video game, but if you find someone who does, find a plane and go where you want.

This is a great idea if the zombie plague is local. If not, you're flying into more trouble anywhere you go. Look for remote landing fields to be the safest. You're also limited in what you can take with you. One checked bag and one carryon isn't going to be enough.

And don't even get me started on the security checks before you can board, huddled like sheep as you wait for someone to look in your shoes. You're pretty much a zombie by the end whether you're bitten or not.

I hate lines.

Abandoned Vehicles

Great place to siphon a little gas when you run low. Toss a couple bucks on the seat, only fair of you. You can also find a tire iron when your axe gets wrenched away from you, you run out of bullets, and your shovel is stuck in some zombie's skull.

Abandoned cars and trucks often contain first aid supplies and flares. You should note that glow sticks are like catnip to zombies. They love them. Flares get their fear instinct going, but glow sticks seem to bring out their curiosity. Zombies like to bite what they're curious about, so don't confuse glow sticks and flares. Though, if you spin and twirl a glow stick sometimes the zombie will get the urge to dance and you can escape. It also helps if you can beat box.

I haven't tried the glow stick technique. I'm sure it'll work... maybe.

The Library

The zombies here are super quiet and polite, but they still bite. I'd still swing by and pick up a few reference books. A military survival guide, scout manual, and a book on edible plants would be high on my list of things to check out.

Weapons

Yay! Weapons!

Firearms

Always a good weapon to have on hand. Most work from a distance. Most do hefty damage. Make sure you aim for the head or the heart. I know, I know, Hollywood told you the head only. That makes no sense and I'll get into it later. These are the two most effective targets on a zombie.

The only downside is you have to have ammo, and the ammo that fits the gun. Unlike movies, you'll have to reload and you'll eventually run out of bullets. Also, unlike video games, you cannot just find ammo stashed all over the ground and under plants and vases. Even if you did, this ammo might not work with your particular firearm.

So, make sure you have plenty of bullets, know how to reload, and can aim decently, or you will get eaten. Oh, and bb guns are not a good choice. They aren't strong enough to do anything more than annoy a zombie and, as with most emotions, zombies bite what annoys them.

Paintball guns are not a good option either. You're not hurting them; you're just painting them pretty colors from a distance. While this may be entertaining, it will not help you in the long run.

Green or Pink, Zombies are still Zombies.

Axes

Axes are always handy. You can crack open a zombies skull, splinter open a locked door, break off an annoying lock on a gate, chop firewood, dice carrots, and even open cans. Just make sure you clean your axe thoroughly before using it on cans or in the kitchen. Cross contamination is bad enough when you're talking salmonella. You don't want to make the same mistake with zombie guts. Like any bladed weapon, it will dull over time and may get stuck in a zombie's ribcage, skull, shin, etc.

Hatchets

This has all the uses of an axe with one bonus and one minus. It's smaller and easier to carry and handle, but that means it's subject to reach restraints. You have to be closer to the zombie to kill it. You don't want to be close to zombies. Yes, you can throw a hatchet from a distance, but then your hatchet is gone. That is not the best use of a weapon, but may come in handy as a last resort.

Fire

As stated earlier, zombies don't like fire. It evokes primal fear center in what is left of their rotting brains. Torches, flares, bonfires, a lot of candles, fiery oil moats are all great ways to keep zombies at bay.

You have little to worry about besides the obvious. Fire is dangerous. You can lose control and burn your whole fortified cabin, distribution center, prison, or whatever down. You can also burn yourself. And if you don't have a first aid kit like I told you to…well, you're not going to be happy. Fire also needs fuel. The fuel runs out and the fire is gone. So, if you're relying on fire, make sure you have plenty of firewood, oil, gas, or whatever else you can burn to keep it going.

Shovels

Shovels, like axes, are one of the most universal weapons. You can use them to beat zombies, dig trenches as barriers or as waste disposal (yes, you need toilets even when hiding from zombies), move coals for cooking, knock boxes off high shelves, bury fire before it gets out of control, dig traps for zombies or food, as a crutch, bury an eaten friend, and more. They have decent reach, weight, and balance. I like shovels more than a little. Try to remember yours

Wood With Nail

This may sound like a good weapon, but really it's not. The nail evokes the memory of pain in a normal human. Most of us have managed to step on a nail at some point in our lives. Zombies don't feel pain the same way. The nail does little good. It just gives the weapon a larger chance of getting stuck two inches deep in some zombie bone, useless to you. I recommend the wood without the nail. You can beat zombies pretty good until the wood breaks.

Table Leg

Zombie piñata anyone?

Table legs are thick, made to withstand the weight of several elbows, even though you know it's rude to rest them there, several buckets of mashed potatoes, a thirty-five pound turkey, three gallons of gravy, ten pounds of wet, nasty bread out of the turkey's rear, a good hundred pounds of ancient china that only sees the light of day once or twice a year, another ten gallons of sparkling cider, ten pounds more of miscellaneous green bean or yam dishes, and at least fifty-five pounds of pie. In other words table legs are strong. They make a pretty effective club with decent reach and weight, can withstand a few skull crushings, and stand up to gnawing pretty well.

Swords

Swords are a little tricky to come by, but can be effective weapons. You want one with a good reach on it. Cut off limbs and the head if possible and you stop zombies cold. Like axes, they'll need some care and attention. Keep them clean and try to sharpen them now and again. They can be a little messy, so keep your mouth closed while swinging.

Knives

I don't recommend using knives. You wind up too close for comfort and too messy. They're nice to have for cooking, but I wouldn't go pulling one out to fight off a zombie mob. Running is more effective.

Bare Hands

All in all a very bad idea, unless you're wearing chainmail over latex, in which case you're okay…though very, very odd.

Teeth

Though this is often a good fighting technique with another human, it's not the brightest thing to try against a zombie. Besides the obvious that you may very well infect yourself, the stupid zombie feels little pain and will not let you go when bitten.

Seriously, if you bite a zombie then you probably deserve what's coming.

Anatomy/Neurology of a Zombie

What do we know about zombies? Undead? Probably not.

Most likely we're looking at a viral infection or neurotoxin that travels through the blood and attacks the brain. This infection moves from host to host through blood and saliva, most often by biting.

Once inside the human body, the virus or toxin travels to the brain and shuts down higher functions and many other control centers. Pain receptors seem to be toast. Zombies can take huge amounts of damage without blinking. Actually, I'm not sure if zombies blink at all.

Communication is fried, except for some moaning. The word "brains" may be the only word left in their vocabulary that can be discerned intelligibly. Even that is highly slurred and they could be saying "brings", "brawns", "barns", and half a dozen other nonsense words.

Still crazy eyes

This drawing turned out a little better.

Sweating stops, no more need for deodorant, though they stink no matter what. Metabolism slows down even more than when you hit thirty. Breathing becomes slow and shallow. Hair and nail growth stops despite what movies tell you. They no longer feel any need to sleep, like your old roommate in college who stayed up late every night watching dumb movies.

The urge to bite the uninfected seems to be all the rave. The act of biting releases hormones into the zombie brain and is the only time you'll see a zombie show pleasure and smile. It would be heartwarming if it wasn't so creepy, painful, and deadly.

The virus or neurotoxin is very specific, crippling half the brain, but leaving the subconscious and some instincts intact. Zombies won't be able to speak, recognize their friends, or juggle, but they'll happily shuffle off to work, school, and their local hangouts.

The ability of the infected to recognize their own kind is flawless. They never attack another zombie, ever. It's rather amazing. You take a group of humans and set them to fighting, someone will accidentally take a swing at a friend, but zombies never do. This implies that the virus gives off some signal that is recognizable to other zombies.

This signal could be a smell, some sort of pheromone, but then you'd expect the zombies to attack anything that didn't have this smell. Dumpsters, buildings, trees would receive equal attention as humans. You would also expect zombies to lose control and attack other zombies as their nasal passages and smell receptors rotted away. We may never know what signal they use to discern human from zombie.

If we could learn to imitate this signal, we could walk through the midst of a crowd of zombies untouched. We could patent it, "eau de zombe" or some such and make millions, though you'd most likely not have much of a sense of smell if you could stomach wearing the stuff.

Since the virus communicates, this implies that it's a smart virus, designed and engineered to be more deadly and widespread. The desire to bite others also supports this theory. The infected are driven to spread the infection as much as possible. In other words…bite, bite, bite.

It's their prime instinct, to search out normal humans and bite them. Yes, an airborne virus would be quicker, but also more dangerous to those releasing such a virus. Plus, the psychological warfare of a zombie virus would be a great advantage in forcing a population to turn on itself.

Is there a cure? I can imagine a future where someone is naturally immune, bitten, catching the virus, managing to overcome it, and creating antibodies. A vaccine could very well be created to inoculate future generations. Unfortunately, the only way to find out if you're immune is to be bitten. I don't recommend trying this little experiment. Running has better odds.

Can a zombie be hurt? Yes and no. They don't feel pain or at least they don't react to pain. You may think this would be nice, especially after dropping an iron on your hand when you were eight, but it's not so great.

Pain's a good thing. It reminds you that you're human and it keeps you from doing massive damage to yourself on accident. So the zombie didn't flinch when you hit it with a shovel. This doesn't imply you haven't done damage to that zombie.

Say you cut off an arm. That arm is no longer attached to the brain and ceases to function. Yay! The zombie will also slowly bleed to death. This will take days as the zombie's metabolism and blood flow have slowed immensely, but it will still die. Don't believe anyone who says there is no blood. Of course there is. Cells need energy to move. Blood carries energy.

If you damage the brain or the heart, death will be quicker. If you cut off a head, the zombie will die pretty much immediately, just avoid the last couple seconds of death biting. If you do enough damage to the body, the zombie will die. The idea that zombies will continue to crawl after you no matter what or a severed limb will inch towards you is creepy and great in movies, but also absurd. So, aim for the head and the chest.

Will a zombie continue to live forever if undamaged? Also false. Do you truly believe everything you see on TV? Muscles contain a finite amount of energy and since zombies don't eat, besides the occasional face of a friend, this energy is not replaced. The muscles will cease to work at a certain point. Also, with the virus destroying the immune system, zombies will be wide open to all manner of illness, disease, plague, and pestilence.

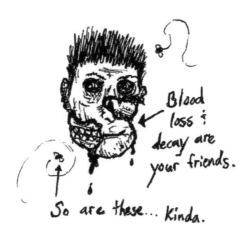

Their lowered metabolism and inability to regulate temperature will make them susceptible to larva, insect, and bacterial infestation. Stick a piece of meat outside for a while and watch what happens to it. Ants and flies are your new best friends in a zombie invasion. Zombies will literally be eaten and rot away in front of you. Gross and stinky, yes, but a good thing in the long run if you want to survive.

Their inability to regulate body temperature also makes them subject to the weather. Extreme heat and extreme cold will kill a zombie. Hot deserts will suck the moisture from a zombie. No moisture, no life. Frosty mountain tops will freeze the blood and cells crack and burst. Dead and dead.

A zombie, even in a lowered metabolic state, needs energy to continue shuffling and moaning. Without much food or liquid, the energy will be cannibalized from the fats in the body, then from the muscle, and eventually from the heart and what's left of the brain. Even though zombies don't attack their own, at least they're eating themselves. Thank you for that, zombies.

The zombies don't sweat and retain much of their water content at the point of infection. Hopefully the sun will still cook some of this moisture off. Leave crates of alcohol around and maybe the zombies will drink it and cook off moisture faster. It works with sauces.

Death by starvation and dehydration may take months as they use very little energy shuffling, moaning, drooling, and occasionally biting, but death will come and it will be sped up by mother nature. That means wait it out long enough and they'll all be dead and you can reclaim civilization.

The only good news out of this whole tragedy is that you'll most likely be able to choose your homes, and I do mean plural, when things calm down. Debt will be a thing of the past. The bad news is you most likely won't have electricity, running water, fast food, grocery stores, or much of a government. Get ready to do your own farming, which is hard work, really hard work.

Appendix 1-A

72 Hour Kit

Food and Water

(A three day supply of food and water, per person, when no refrigeration or cooking is available)

- Protein/Granola Bars
- Trail Mix/Dried Fruit
- Crackers/Cereals (for munching...no munching on brains)
- Canned Tuna, Beans, Turkey, Beef, Sausages, etc ("pop-top" cans that open without a can-opener might not be a good idea, they can pop open during travel and we all know zombies are attracted to cheap sausage.)
- Canned Juice
- Candy/Gum (warning: some candy can melt and using mint gum might make everything taste like mint. Mint stew, mint clothing, mint bouillon.)
- Water (1 Gallon/4 Liters Per Person)

Bedding and Clothing

- Change of Clothing (short and long sleeved shirts, pants, jackets, socks, etc. Always a good thing to have because you will be stinky and dirty and covered in zombie juice.)
- Undergarments (yes undies are very important, especially since you may soil yours several times while escaping)
- Rain Coat/Poncho (handy for rain or makeshift tents)
- Blankets and Emergency Heat Blanks (that keep in warmth)

- Cloth Sheet (for sleeping, carrying things in a bundle over your shoulder, like Santa, and for cutting into ribbons for bandages and such)
- Plastic Sheet (makeshift shelter...will not keep zombies out)

Fuel and Light

- Battery Lighting (Flashlights, Lamps, etc.) Don't forget batteries!
- Extra Batteries (do not keep them stored in the flashlights)
- Flares (zombies do not like flares)
- Candles (zombies do not like fire in general)
- Lighter (zombies no likey)
- Water-Proof Matches (fire bad to zombies...also useful for cooking)

Equipment

- Can Opener (if you forgot this one...good luck beating those cans open with a rock)
- Dishes/Utensils (because we are more civilized than zombies)
- Shovel (very useful as a tool and a weapon)
- Radio (with batteries!)
- Pen and Paper (this book counts as extra paper if not in ebook form)
- Axe (also useful as a tool and a weapon)
- Pocket Knife (mainly a tool, I wouldn't want to face a zombie armed only with a pocket knife)
- Rope (this is a tool and not much of a weapon)
- Duct Tape (it may save you after all)
- Solar or crank charger (a must have if this guide is on your ebook or cell phone)

Personal Supplies and Medication

- First Aid Kit and Supplies (I have another list below of what should be in this)
- Toiletries (roll of toilet paper- remove the center tube to easily flatten into a zip-lock bag, feminine hygiene, folding brush, etc. You want to be pretty for the zombies.)
- Cleaning Supplies (mini hand sanitizer, soap, shampoo, dish soap, etc. Warning: Scented soap might "flavor" food items. Hand sanitizer is a must after fighting zombies.)
- Immunizations Up-to Date (for bird flu and zombinella)
- Medication (Acetaminophen, Ibuprofen, children's medication, anti-zombie tablets, etc.)
- Prescription Medication (for 3 days)

Personal Documents and Money
(Place these items in a water-proof container!)

- Scriptures (great reading material to keep your mind off zombies)
- Genealogy Records (proves you do not have zombie ancestors)
- Legal Documents (Birth/Marriage Certificates, Wills, Passports, Contracts, etc)
- Vaccination Papers
- Insurance Policies (is zombie attack covered?)

I doubt it...

- Cash (helpful at first, but may decrease in value quickly)
- Credit Card (also helpful at first...as long as there is electricity)
- Pre-Paid Phone Cards

Miscellaneous

- Bag(s) to put 72 Hour Kit items in (such as duffel bags or back packs, which work great) Make sure you can

lift/carry/roll it! (they also come in handy once they're empty)
- Infant Needs (if applicable)

Notes:

1. Update your 72 Hour Kit every six months (put a note in your calendar/planner) to make sure that: all food, water, and medication are fresh and have not expired; clothing fits; personal documents and credit cards are up to date; and batteries are charged. (don't be lazy)
2. Small toys/games are important too as they will provide some comfort and entertainment during a stressful time. (There is nothing like a game of go fish to keep your mind off the zombie hordes gathering outside.)
3. Older children can be responsible for their own pack of items/clothes too.
4. You can include any other items in your 72 Hour Kit that you feel are necessary for your family's survival. (axe, guns, flares, glow sticks)
5. Some items and/or flavors might leak, melt, "flavor" other items, or break open. Dividing groups of items into individual zipping bags might help prevent this.

Zombies are stinky enough. Try not to pack super fragrancy stuff.

↑ So a word.

Appendix 1-B

First Aid Kit and Supplies

- Container (metal, wood, or plastic) with a fitted cover to store first aid kit
- First Aid Booklet (including CPR, DO NOT attempt CPR on a Zombie!)
- Prescribed Medications
- Any critical medical family histories (susceptibility to zombie strain)
- Adhesive (as in tape, you dummy)
- Ammonia (zombies do not like ammonia)
- Bicarbonate of soda (for upset stomach...which may be often)
- Calamine lotion (sunburn/insect and zombie bites)
- Diarrhea remedy (from not boiling your water, silly)
- Elastic bandages
- Gauze bandages
- Hot-water bottle (don't know why...)
- Hydrogen peroxide (for use on zombie bites)
- Ipecac syrup (induces vomiting, like you're going to need to induce it)
- Knife (not for fighting zombies)
- Matches (fire is your friend)
- Measuring cup (very helpful for making special anti-zombie ramen)

Pretty much the same as regular ramen.

- Medicine dropper
- Needles (for sewing up zombie bites)

- Paper bags (put over head and you are invisible to zombies for three minutes)

I haven't tested this one either. It may only work for three seconds... or hours. Three of something anyway. Perhaps...

- Razor blades
- Rubbing alcohol (dump on zombie bites)
- Safety pins
- Scissors
- Soap (wash hands often during zombie invasions)
- Thermometer (zombies do not have a stable temperature)
- Triangular bandages (you don't want round ones)
- Tweezers (for eyebrows...crazy eyebrows make zombies angry)
- Prescriptions

Additional First Aid Kit Supplies

- Immunization records
- Medications for children (if applicable)
- Fever reducing medications such as aspirin, acetaminophen, or ibuprofen
- Allergy medication (I'm allergic to zombies, may work...you never know)
- Antibacterial wipes
- Antibiotic ointment
- Antiseptic wipes

- Band-aids (for zombie boo-boos)

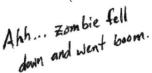
Ahh... Zombie fell down and went boom.

- Burn ointment/spray (for that iron you dropped on your hand)
- Cotton balls (they squeak when you pull them apart)

My sister hates this sound.

- Cough syrup/cough drops (sore throat is an early symptom of zombiness)
- Disposable blanket (why are we throwing things away)
- Eye drops/eye wash (red eyes and someone may mistake you for a zombie)
- Feminine Hygiene
- Latex Gloves (yeah...a must have. Wear under chain-mail gloves)
- Hand sanitizer (use often after fighting zombies)
- Hot and cold instant packs
- Hydrocortisone cream
- Lip ointment (chap stick, pucker up for the zombies)
- Medical tape (waterproof & regular)
- Nail clippers (zombies are jealous of long nails, keep them trim)
- Needle and thread (sewing is a nice past time)
- Snake bite kit (also known as zombie bite kit...a must have as well)
- Sterile strips
- Sunscreen/lotion (you don't want a sunburn while running from the mindless hordes)
- Tourniquet kit (may keep zombie bite from spreading)
- Petroleum Jelly (zombies do not like this goopy stuff, spread it all over your arms and legs)
- Water purification tablets (duh!)

Notes:

1. Update your first aid kit every six months (put a note in your calendar/planner) to replenish and check all supplies. Expired or contaminated items should be replaced. (don't be lazy)
2. Check with your family doctor for any specific medicines and first aid supplies your family might require for an emergency.
3. Some items may leak or break open. Using tubes, plastic bottles, or zipping bags can help prevent contamination.
4. All first aid supplies should be labeled and organized for quick and easy use.
5. Supplies may be divided and organized into compartments or sections for easier access when using your first aid kit.
6. You may include any other first aid items you feel would be useful or necessary.
7. A condensed version of this first aid kit should also be included in your 72 hour kit.

About the Author

Charles M. Pulsipher lives in Saint George Utah with his lovely wife and neurotic dog. He writes sci-fi and fantasy with the occasional zombie guide thrown in. He's obsessed with surviving the zombie-pocalypse.

He draws cartoons on his blog that are usually funny if lacking in the amazingly artistic department. http://noticeyourworld.blogspot.com/

He spends his time away from the keyboard hiking and camping in stunning Southern Utah.

He neglects his twitter account. @charliepulse

You can email him with questions, typos, concerns, and for news at raptorbark@hotmail.com

His velociraptor impression is worth seeing, even if it makes grown-ups scream and hide. It's probably the coolest thing about him.

Also Look For

Made in the USA
Lexington, KY
15 July 2012